# Soccer

## A Level One Reader

By Cynthia Klingel and Robert B. Noyed

The Child's World®

It is time to go to my soccer game.

I have pads to protect
my legs.

I have my uniform
and shoes.

We play soccer on a grassy field.

Each team has ten players on the field.

We can kick the ball
with our feet.

We can bump the ball
with our heads.

Each team tries to kick the ball into the goal.

The goalie tries to stop
the ball.

My game is over. I am tired, but I had fun.

# Word List

field

goalie

kick

protect

uniform

# Note to Parents and Educators

Welcome to The Wonders of Reading™! These books provide text at three different levels for beginning readers to practice and strengthen their reading skills. Additionally, the use of nonfiction text provides readers the valuable opportunity to *read to learn*, not just to learn to read.

These leveled readers allow children to choose books at their level of reading confidence and performance. Level One books offer beginning readers simple language, word choice, and sentence structure as well as a word list. Level Two books feature slightly more difficult vocabulary, longer sentences, and longer total text. In the back of each Level Two book are an index and a list of books and Web sites for finding out more information. Level Three books continue to extend word choice and length of text. In the back of each Level Three book are a glossary, an index, and a list of books and Web sites for further research.

State and national standards in reading and language arts emphasize using nonfiction at all levels of reading development. The Wonders of Reading™ fill the historical void in nonfiction material for the primary grade readers with the additional benefit of a leveled text.

# About the Authors

Cindy Klingel has worked as a high school English teacher and an elementary teacher. She is currently the curriculum director for a Minnesota school district. Writing children's books is another way for her to continue her passion for sharing the written word with children. Cindy Klingel is a frequent visitor to the children's section of bookstores and enjoys spending time with her many friends, family, and two daughters.

Bob Noyed started his career as a newspaper reporter. Since then, he has worked in communications and public relations for more than fourteen years for a Minnesota school district. He enjoys writing books for children and finds that it brings a different feeling of challenge and accomplishment from other writing projects. He is an avid reader who also enjoys music, theater, traveling, and spending time with his wife, son, and daughter.

**Published by The Child's World®, Inc.**
PO Box 326
Chanhassen, MN 55317-0326
800-599-READ
www.childsworld.com

With special thanks to the American Youth Soccer Association
of Chicago, the Almeida Family, Coach Hansen, Referee Pletz,
and the Dolphins soccer team for providing the modeling and
location for this book.

**Photo Credits**
All photos © Flanagan Publishing Services/Romie Flanagan

Project Coordination: Editorial Directions, Inc.
Photo Research: Alice K. Flanagan

**Library of Congress Cataloging-in-Publication Data**
Klingel, Cynthia Fitterer.
Soccer / by Cynthia Klingel and Robert B. Noyed.
p.  cm.  —  (Wonder books)
"A level one reader" —Cover.
Summary: Illustrations and simple text describe the fun a child has playing soccer.
ISBN 1-56766-805-4 (lib. reinforced : alk. paper)
1. Soccer—Juvenile literature.    [1. Soccer.]
I. Noyed, Robert B.    II. Title.    III. Wonder books (Chanhassen, Minn.)

GV943.25 .K55          2000
796.334—dc21           99-057410